Fortune Cookie

MIRROR,
MIRROR...

FORTUNE TELLERS Club

MIRROR, MIRROR...

DOTTI ENDERLE

Llewellyn Publications
St. Paul, Minnesota

FIRST EDITION
First printing, 2004

Book design and editing by Kimberly Nightingale
Cover design by Kevin R. Brown
Cover illustration and interior illustrations © 2004 by Matthew
   Archambault

Library of Congress Cataloging-in-Publication Data
Enderle, Dotti, 1954–
      Mirror, mirror— / Dotti Enderle.— 1st ed.
         p. cm. — (Fortune tellers club ; 6)
      Summary: When twelve-year-old Gena starts to see an unknown
girl with pigtails and a uni-eyebrow reflected in her mirror, she and
the other Fortune Tellers Club members try to discover the girl's
identity and somehow recover Gena's reflection.
      ISBN: 0-7387-0436-9
      [1. Supernatural—Fiction. 2. Mirrors—Fiction. 3. Clubs—Fiction.] I. Title.
Pz7.E69645Mi 2004
[Fic]—dc22   2004044206

Llewellyn Publications
A Division of Llewellyn Worldwide, Ltd.
P.O. Box 64383, Dept. 0-7387-0436-9
St. Paul, MN 55164-0383, U.S.A.
www.llewellyn.com

Printed in the United States of America

Other Books by Dotti Enderle

The Lost Girl
Playing with Fire
The Magic Shades
Secrets of Lost Arrow
Hand of Fate

Contents

CHAPTER 1

Staring Back

*M*eow. Gena stirred in her sleep, dreaming of cotton candy sticking to her chin.

Meow.

More cotton candy. She just couldn't seem to keep it in her mouth. It grew wetter and stickier and . . . *meow.*

She woke up to a pair of shiny mismatched eyes staring into hers. "Shhhh, Twilight!" she said, cuddling the cat close. "We'll get busted for sure."

The cat continued to lick her chin. "Okay, okay."

Meow.

She heard stirring in the next room. "Shhhh!" After opening the window, she picked up the cat and lightly dropped him outside. "Bye-bye, Twilight."

She watched as he stretched, then moseyed off for the day. Quickly, she sprayed the room with the "Freshness of Mountain Air," then hid the air freshener in a drawer. Another night without getting caught. *Great!* She headed off to breakfast.

"You're up early again," her dad said as she entered the kitchen.

"Yeah. Well . . . you know." She walked around him to get the cereal from the pantry.

"It's just that you're not usually an early riser. Are you really my daughter, or is this one of those *Invasion of the Body Snatchers* scenarios?"

"Trust me, Dad, it's me. I only let the aliens take over when I'm bored in class."

He snickered as he poured another cup of coffee. "I'm off to work."

Gena looked at the clock. Wow, it *was* early, even for a school morning. She relaxed as she ate her breakfast, then went to the bathroom to brush her teeth. She wet the brush, squeezed on some toothpaste, and grinned toward the mirror. *What?* Her heart jumped a high hurdle, and she stumbled back, dropping the icky toothpaste off her brush. The reflection in the mirror wasn't hers.

She stared forward, taking a moment to catch her breath. Was she still asleep? That had to be it. She was never up this early anyway, so it must be a dream. She pinched herself hard. "Ouch!" *Okay, not a dream.* She inched forward and so did the reflection. Gena looked down at the green tee shirt she wore with the words *Girls Kick Butt* on the front. Peeking up, she saw that her reflection had been staring down at a neatly pressed white shirt. Gena touched the mirror. Who was this? For a moment she thought she'd faint.

She clamped her eyes shut, her heart pounding wildly. *I'm not crazy. I'm not crazy.* She slowly opened her eyes. *I'm not cra . . . uuuuuuuughhhhhhhh!*

The strange reflection still lingered. Long blond hair in braids, tiny nose, uni-brow. *Yuck! Buy some tweezers, girl!*

This was clearly not Gena, but the reflection moved as though it was—every single, teeny-tiny maneuver.

There's a logical explanation. This is too freaky to be real. It's a trick! "Ah ha!" Gena shouted. She scrambled around, looking for a camera. "You don't fool me. This is really just a glass window, and I'm on one of those lame hidden camera shows. All right, where is it? And where's the microphone. Come on, I hate reality TV!"

Gena used her peripheral vision to watch as the reflection looked for the camera too. And the girl's mouth moved with every word Gena spoke. "Not cool," Gena said, tapping on the glass.

She left the bathroom, walked back to her bedroom, and felt a ripple of shock when the girl occupied her dresser mirror too. "This is impossible. I look like one of the preppy girls at school, only with one eyebrow." Her heart still raced, but she was determined to stay calm.

Gena went into her dad's bedroom, his bath-room, and even found an old hand mirror to check herself out. All the same.

She wilted across her bed, shivering, afraid to look anymore. This had to be some sort of joke. No, the joke came when she looked at the alarm clock. 7:45. Great, only fifteen minutes to get dressed and off to school. She kept her back to the mirror and brushed her teeth. She stumbled out of the bathroom and avoided the bedroom mirror as she got dressed.

Even though she was alone in the house, she felt like that reflection, whoever she was, was watching her. She shuffled all her books and papers into her backpack and headed for the front door. Wait! Gena stamped her foot as she remembered that she hadn't brushed her hair. *So what else is new?* she thought, running her fingers through it. But the ends were plastered together from being too close to her chin while Twilight had given her a tongue bath. "Arrrrgh!" It had to be brushed.

I can do this without looking. She threw her hair up in a ponytail, but felt a cowlick sticking up near the side. She pulled out the elastic band and tried again.

"It would help if I could see what I was doing!" Gena hoped the reflection could hear that. Another cowlick. *Yuck!* She pulled the ponytail down and brushed her hair hard. This time it went up smoothly. As a natural reflex, she glanced toward the mirror. *Ick!* Maybe Dad was right. This must be a case of the Body Snatchers.

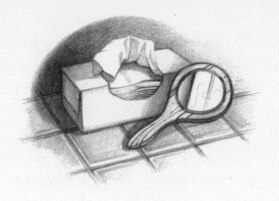

CHAPTER 2

Sniffles and Sneers

Gena didn't bother to lock her bike. She hurried into the school, and headed straight for the attendance office, no note of course. Mrs. Durwood, the attendance clerk, was on the phone. She glanced up at Gena and shook her head. Gena knew that gesture. It meant *Tsk! Tsk! Late again.*

Behind Mrs. Durwood's desk was a large framed photo of the school. Gena never understood why they needed a picture of it when they could just step outside and look. But someone must have used extra glass cleaner when cleaning the dust off. It reflected everything in the office, including her. Okay, not her—but it should have been her. Even with the glare of the fluorescent lights on the glass, she could tell it was Miss Pigtails, looking disgusted right back at her.

"Gena, what happened?" Mrs. Durwood asked, hanging up the phone. "You've been so punctual lately."

Gena shrugged. No explanation was better than the whopper she'd concocted, just in case. She took the tardy notice. "Thank you."

As she turned to leave Mrs. Durwood called, "Oh, and you have something on your lip."

Gena knocked it off. A piece of dried cereal. Thank goodness it wasn't a booger. The things you miss when you have no reflection.

She ran up the stairs, but quickly buckled to a fast walk when she saw a teacher leaving the Xerox room. She hurried to class, dropped the tardy note on the teacher's desk, then scooted into her seat like no one would notice. So much for creeping in like a mouse. The room froze when she came in and twenty-four pairs of eyes watched her every move. *At least* you *can see me!* she wanted to scream at them.

"We're on page 277," Mr. Douglas said.

Gena fumbled in her backpack and pulled out her book. Mr. Douglas continued his lecture. She tried to hurry, to play catch-up with the lesson, but Beth Wilson was making the most distracting nasal noises behind her. *Get a Kleenex!* Gena thought. She slapped at the pages of her science book with her fingers, fanning them back in clumps. *277! 277!* More sniffles behind her. This was just too weird. Gena pretended to drop a piece of paper so she could see what all the sobbing was about. Beth's forehead rested on her hands, as though she were trying to hide her face. Gena heard a teeny wince escape.

She sat back up and turned to page 277. *Oh great.* A lovely picture of a human brain. Maybe that's why Beth was crying. She was finally learning in seventh grade that other people had something she didn't. The sniffles increased in magnitude, and bordered just on the edge of disgusting. Gena felt guilty for the "no brains" thought.

More suppressed squeaks. Gena turned around. "Are you okay?" she whispered.

"Mind your own business!" Beth snapped back in a low wet slur.

"Fine." Gena turned back around. That's when she noticed Nicole Hoffman, Snotty Twin number two, eyes and nose a scarlet red. *What's up with that? Did they lose their reflections too?* The day those girls couldn't hog a mirror would be a national day of mourning . . . for them.

"Our brain has two hemispheres," Mr. Douglas droned. "A right brain, and a left brain. Who can tell me the function of each?"

As usual, no one raised their hand. After a pause, Mr. Douglas said, "Gena."

Darn! He always did this to her when she was late. She tried incorporating both her left and right brain to concoct an answer. "Well . . . the left side of the brain stores up stuff like math and science and . . . and . . . learning stuff, like that. The right side stores up dreams and stuff." She chewed her thumbnail, waiting for his lecture on how she should actually read the assigned chapter.

"That's right," Mr. Douglas said, not sounding surprised. "The left side of our brain is the logical part, and the right side is the creative part." Gena wondered which part caused her to think that up in a hurry.

Beth's sniffles were growing just too annoying. *Must be about a boy. Or maybe she stubbed her toe and can't cheer at the game this week. Or maybe it's something worse.* Gena turned around again. "Can I get you a tissue or something?" She hated being nice to Beth, but that continuous train of mucus-snorting was really climbing up her nerves. They'd called Beth and Nicole the Snotty Twins for years, but did they have to literally live up to the name?

Beth didn't answer. She reached for her purse and snuck out her hand mirror. She hovered behind Gena so Mr. Douglas wouldn't see. That's when Gena got a really good look at her. *Uck!* No wonder she was hiding her face. Her forehead and cheeks were blotchy. Her nose was the color of a lobster, and her eyes were practically swollen shut.

"Guess you and your freaky fortune teller friend Juniper can celebrate now," Beth said, wiping her nose with a major pinch of her fingers. She rubbed the back of her hand across the bottoms of her eyes, smudging her already smeared mascara even more.

"Celebrate?" Gena whispered. Could Beth really have good news for her?

Beth drooped closer to the small mirror. "I found out last night that my dad is taking a job in Dallas. We're moving away."

Holding back a smile was like holding back a tornado. "That's tough," Gena said. *For the people in Dallas!* She really wanted to say that out loud, but Beth was so distraught it would have been like picking on someone smaller than her.

Mr. Douglas still lectured. "When using the left side of the brain, you tend to think your thoughts, whereas with the right, you tend to *feel* them." Gena figured she must be using her right brain at the moment because she didn't think she could feel any happier about Beth leaving.

Gena twisted closer. "So when are you going?"

"Be gone!" Beth said, flipping the mirror around to block Gena's face. Gena flinched when Miss Pigtails suddenly appeared before her.

She spun back around to find Mr. Douglas standing right next to her desk. "Let me remind you, Miss Richmond, that your left brain is the side you should be using when in this class. In order to use the left side of your brain, you'll have to pay attention to me and the paragraphs of the text book. You may use your right brain in detention this afternoon."

Detention? *Aarrrrrrgh!* Detention! Gena wondered if she could get Miss Pigtails to show up in her place.

CHAPTER 3

Prove It!

It was lunchtime before Gena got a chance to talk to Anne and Juniper. She leaned in over her food tray so she wouldn't have to shout over the usual cafeteria din. "I've got something to tell you, but you're not going to believe it."

"We heard," Anne said. "Beth is moving to Dallas."

Gena shook her head. "No—"

"Yes," Juniper interrupted. "She's going to Dallas. Do you realize how far away that is? Hours!

15

We'll probably never see her again." Gena could hear the delight in Juniper's voice.

"Yes, I heard she's going to Dallas. But that's not the big deal."

Anne grinned. "Not a big deal? I thought you'd be up doing the happy dance or something. You hate Beth."

Gena slumped. "I know. And she can take her snotty twin with her too as far as I'm concerned, but I have something even more heavy-duty to tell you."

Juniper stopped chewing, and Anne froze on the spot. "What?" Anne asked.

"I've lost my reflection."

The two girls stayed in the same position, only now they looked confused. "I mean . . . I can't see it . . . my reflection . . . when I look in the mirror. I see somebody else."

"What?" Anne said again.

Gena felt agitated. How could she possibly explain this? "This morning when I looked into the bathroom mirror, it wasn't me looking back."

Juniper giggled. "Uh huh, maybe it's time to wash all the toothpaste splatter and zit juice off the mirror."

"I know it sounds insane."

Anne picked up her juice box. "No, it doesn't *sound* insane. It *is* insane." She took a sip, shaking her head.

Gena knew she should have waited. "Okay, fine. I'll just have to prove it to you. Got a mirror? Anne?"

"I don't have my purse with me right now."

Gena looked around the table in search of something reflective. She picked up a spoon and glanced into the curved bowl of it. Miss Pigtails looked back at her, upside down! The spoon was too small anyway. She needed something bigger. Popping a tater tot into her mouth, she let out a sigh. "I'll have to show you after lunch. We'll go to the restroom."

"You're serious," Juniper said, looking Gena straight in the eyes.

"As serious as Beth." Gena nodded toward the end of the table where Beth sat, crying into her peanut butter and jelly. Nicole sat next to her, patting her back and making strange whimpering noises.

"Seeing someone else in the mirror sounds more serious," Anne said. "Why aren't you crying like that?"

"What good would it do?" Gena asked. "I'd only get a runny nose and teary eyes, and no way to see how to wipe either of them."

"I can't wait," Anne said. "Let's go to the restroom right now!" She nearly toppled her tray bouncing up.

"Hold on!" Juniper got up too.

The three girls left the cafeteria and turned into the closest restroom marked *Girls*. As they stepped in, two girls were standing by the sinks, brushing their hair and chatting about boys.

Juniper and Anne went straight to the sinks and looked in the mirrors. Gena hung back by the entrance. No way was she going to take a chance. The last thing she needed was those girls seeing her reflection . . . or whatever she should call it now.

Anne washed her hands, and Juniper fidgeted about. Finally, the girls walked out, still jabbering about which boys were cool and which were jerks.

"Are you ready?" Gena asked.

Juniper and Anne didn't look ready. They looked anxious. Gena's heartbeat quickened. She suddenly felt anxious too. This was the first time anyone else would see it. She walked to the sinks and peeked in. Before she could even get a good glance, Anne screamed like she'd just seen Frank-enstein leave a stall. Juniper clamped her hand over Anne's mouth to keep her from screaming some more. Gena was about ready to scream too. Miss Pigtails was still there, only now one of her braids was frayed and saggy. It bushed out like her eyebrows. She looked upset.

"Who is that?" Juniper said, her eyes bright as headlights.

"How should I know?" Gena asked. "I was hoping *you'd* tell *me*."

Anne mumbled something under Juniper's hand. Her eyes looked doubled in size too.

"What?" Juniper asked, lowering her hand.

"It's got to be a trick," Anne repeated more coherently.

"It's not a very funny one," Gena said.

The girls moved in closer to Gena and all three stared at the reflections. "What's with the plaid skirt?" Juniper asked.

Gena slumped. "I look like Heidi."

Anne squirmed. "No, you look more like that Swiss Miss Chocolate girl."

"Why me?" Gena said, shaking her head. She'd been wondering that all morning. It felt good to finally voice it.

"Or more importantly," Juniper added, "Why?"

Anne tapped the mirror. "How?"

Gena shrugged. "Whatever."

Juniper leaned on the sink and crossed her arms. "What are we going to do?"

Gena was relieved to hear Juniper ask that. She wasn't in this alone.

"Weird things call for weird measures," Anne said. "There's obviously some metaphysical or cosmic explanation for this."

Juniper nodded. "You're right. We definitely need to have a Fortune Tellers Club meeting. Right after school."

"Well . . . not *right* after," Gena said. "How about an hour after school?"

"Do you have detention?" Anne asked. "Gena!"

"Hey, give me a break," Gena said, looking back toward the mirror. "I'm not myself today."

Juniper laughed. "You can say that again!"

More girls came in and the Fortune Tellers Club slipped out. They took their seats at the table, eating in a hurry. "We'll meet at my house," Gena said. "Just in case we need to do some kind of exorcism on the mirrors."

Anne dropped her sandwich. "We may have to do one on *you*! What if you're possessed by that girl, and you can see your soul in the mirror?"

Gena stopped eating and looked at her hands. She touched her face. "But I still feel like me. I still think like me. If I was possessed, wouldn't I be talking in some strange language and spitting up pea soup?"

"Not if you were worried about getting it on your starchy white blouse," Juniper said with a giggle.

Gena gave her a look. "Trust me. I'm still in here."

Just then someone leaned in front of her. "Hi, Juniper." It was Nicole, her face slightly puffy and pink. "Since we have dance class tonight, I was thinking maybe we could give you a ride. My mom could come and pick you up."

Gena watched the confusion circling Juniper's face. "I have a ride," she said.

"I know," Nicole said. "But since we're going to be doing a lot of rehearsing together, we might want to car pool. It'll be fun."

It will? Gena thought.

Juniper smiled. "Maybe next week. I think my mom's going to take me to McDonald's first, then we have to drop Jonathan off at ball practice. Things are all set right now."

Nicole gave her a sugary smile. "Okay. Next week." She walked off.

"What nerve!" Gena said, ready to explode. She'd always known Nicole was two-faced.

"Yeah," Juniper agreed. "Beth is leaving. Now Nicole needs a new friend."

Gena giggled. "Maybe I should hand her a mirror and introduce her to Miss Pigtails."

All three snickered as they dumped their trash and rushed off to their next class.

CHAPTER 4

Mirror Gazing

Gena spent her hour in detention trying to use her left brain. Her logical brain. The brain that would be able to deduce the problem, and give her a good solid answer about why this was all happening to her. She tried to figure it out, but in the end, her right brain won, and she spent a good deal of time staring out the window and daydreaming.

Gena crept into the apartment about 4:30 p.m. She could hear Rachael, her dad's girlfriend, humming in the kitchen.

"Gena, is that you?"

Gena stuck her head around the doorway and peeked in. Rachael stood at the stove stirring something in a large pot.

"Give me a hand, will you? I need to make the salad."

Gena trudged over to the stove, not sure if she wanted to help. Rachael had turned out to be a superior cook, and Gena didn't want to mess anything up. "What do you need me to do?"

"Just stir this sauce so it doesn't stick to the pot." Rachael grabbed some lettuce out of the fridge, and began vigorously tearing it to shreds and dropping the pieces into a bowl.

Gena stirred. Whatever was in that pot with the noodles smelled heavenly. She leaned toward it to take a good sniff. That's when she realized that the stainless-steel pot was as shiny as a mirror. Her reflection bounced right off it, a tiny bit distorted, but a reflection indeed. Only Gena really wished it was her reflection. Miss Pigtails looked kind of funny on the concave shape of the pot. Her nose looked like a punching bag hanging just below that hairy caterpillar of an eyebrow. Her braids were long and skinny like two pretzel sticks. *Just what you deserve for taking over my reflection!* Gena thought, trying not to laugh out loud at the funny image on the pot.

Rachael turned around. "How's the stirring coming along?"

"Great," Gena said, trying to stay in between Rachael and the image of Miss Pigtails shining off the pot. When Rachael went back to the refrigerator, Gena scooted over a bit. When Rachael went back to the counter, Gena scooted the other way. No way could Rachael see this. She might freak out! Then Gena noticed Miss Pigtails reflected in the toaster too. She laid down the spoon and grabbed a dishtowel. She quietly snuck over and draped the dishtowel over the toaster. That's when she saw *her* on the metal flour canister. *Aaarrrrgh!* Miss Pigtails was like an irritating Tinkerbell flitting from shine to shine. Gena wished she had a flyswatter. She'd love to run around the kitchen slapping at all the images of Miss Pigtails like the pesky little bug she'd turned out to be. But instead of a flyswatter, Gena leaned a pot-holder against the canister to hide its gleam.

A sudden spout of steam, followed by the sound of dripping globs had Gena whipping back around. The sauce had bubbled over and drooled down the pot like a volcano.

"Gena! You were supposed to be stirring." Rachael grabbed a cloth and wiped the side of the pan as she quickly stirred.

Gena sighed with relief. The mess had made a sticky film on the pot, covering the reflection. "Do you still want me to stir?"

"That's okay. I'm just going to let it simmer a bit more, then get the salad ready before I go to work." Rachael hurried about the kitchen.

Gena started for her room, then turned back. "Sorry about the stirring. And thanks for cooking dinner for Dad and me."

Rachael smiled. "Just save me some, okay?" She winked.

Gena had barely made it to her room when she heard the doorbell. "I got it!" She let Juniper and Anne in, and they rushed quietly and secretively to her bedroom.

"Can you still see her?" Juniper asked.

"Oh yeah! And she looks worse every time I look."

"What should we do?" Anne asked.

"I thought about breaking all the mirrors, but each one would bring seven years bad luck. If I break all the mirrors, I'm looking at a lifetime of misfortune. I'm having enough rotten luck as it is."

"Look on the bright side," Juniper said. "Even though you've lost your reflection and you landed detention, it won't be long until Beth moves. I'd say that's a real plus."

Gena stretched out, resting her head on her hand. "Yeah, but I'd enjoy it even more if I could see myself grinning."

"Then lets get to the bottom of this," Anne suggested. "We need to find out who that girl is."

Juniper nodded. "I think we should try crystal gazing again. Only this time we won't use a bowl of water."

"I don't have a crystal ball," Gena said, laying down flat on the floor and staring at the ceiling. "You could use my dad's bowling ball. It's a pukey yellow with these weird 3-D swirls all over it. It looks magical."

"I'm not going to try gazing in a bowling ball!" Juniper said. "How dumb is that!"

Gena snickered. "You're right. You'd probably strike out anyway."

Anne moaned and Juniper shook her head. "I think we should go straight to the source of the problem," Juniper said.

Gena glanced over. "Which is?"

"A mirror! Let's try scrying in a mirror."

Anne bounced where she sat. "I think that's a perfect idea."

"You would," Gena said. "You always know who's gazing back."

"You don't have to look," Juniper assured her. "Anne and I will try it."

Gena didn't say a word. Instead she got up and went to the bathroom to retrieve a mirror that would work. Under the sink was a large hand mirror about the size of a salad plate. A flat crystal ball. She held it away so she couldn't see in. "Here you go."

Juniper took the mirror and set it down between herself and Anne. Gena scrunched into a corner and hugged her knees.

Juniper and Anne leaned in, accidentally bumping heads. "Ouch!" They tried again.

Gena watched both girls staring hard in the mirror. Neither said a word. "Do you see anything?"

Juniper looked up and rubbed her eyes. "I think maybe you should look in too."

"Why?" Gena asked. "Won't it be crowded with the extra reflection?"

Juniper motioned her over. "Come on. If we back up a little, and only look at the girl's reflection in the mirror, maybe we can tell something about her."

Gena trudged over in a slow crawl. "Whatever." She looked in. Miss Pigtails looked angry. Her eyes were narrowed, making her eyebrows look even bigger and shaggier. "Okay, Pippi Longstocking, what have you done with my reflection?"

The three girls stared down, and the girl in the mirror stared back. Gena didn't blink. Maybe now she'd find out something. It was like a staredown. The first one to blink loses. Gena wasn't going to lose. She stared hard. She imagined Miss Pigtails vanishing in a *poof* of smoke, and her own reflection taking her place. It'd be just like magic. She leaned in closer. So did Anne and Juniper, now reflected too. So many eyes fixed on the mirror. Suddenly, a strange face appeared in the mirror. Juniper and Anne screamed.

Gena's heart rippled, then she realized it was just Twilight, nosing in to take a look too.

"A cat?" Anne said. "When did you get a cat?"

"*How* did you get a cat?" Juniper asked.

"Shhhh." Gena picked up Twilight and rubbed his neck. "He just wandered up here, looking hungry. I've had him for a couple of weeks now, but it's getting tougher to keep him hidden."

"Look at his eyes," Anne said. "One's light blue and one's dark gray."

Gena grinned. "Wicked, huh? That's why I named him Twilight. His eyes are the color of the twilight sky."

A rap on the door made them jump again. "Gena, I'm going to work now. When your dad gets home, you'll need to reheat the strudel. Everything else is ready. The salad's in the fridge."

The Fortune Tellers Club all sat, frozen in their spots. "Okay, thanks," Gena called out. She let out a nervous breath as she heard Rachael leave. "That was close."

"How do you manage to keep this cat hidden from the apartment manager?" Juniper asked.

"That's the easy part," Gena said. "The hard part is keeping him hidden from my dad!"

Meow. Twilight slipped out of Gena's arms and curled up on top of the mirror.

"Guess we won't be doing any more mirror gazing today," Anne said with a smile.

"It wasn't working anyway," Juniper said. "But I have another idea. Let me look in some of my books at home, and I'll call you."

Gena shrugged. "In the meantime I'll take Twilight's suggestion and cover all the mirrors."

Juniper and Anne left, and Gena curled up next to her cat. She closed her eyes and stroked his fur. The smoothness eased her into a peaceful calm. But after a minute she opened her eyes and sat up with a jerk. "Whoa . . . Twilight . . . how did *you* get inside?"

CHAPTER 5

Another Surprise

Gena woke up from some weird dreams. The places and people in them were familiar, but she wasn't. In every dream she was the strange girl in braids, walking, talking, and carrying on just as Gena would. And Twilight flashed on and off like the Cheshire Cat in *Alice in Wonderland.* "I may go completely loco!" Gena cried, sitting up and yawning.

Something moved under the covers. "Come here." She pulled Twilight out and scratched his ears. "Hungry?"

She went through the morning routine of feeding him, emptying the litter, and secretly saying goodbye. When she slipped him out of the window, she double-checked the lock. If things weren't confusing enough in the last twenty-four hours, she was still pondering on how Twilight had gotten into the apartment yesterday.

She brushed her teeth and hair with her eyes closed, and made it to school just as the bell rang. When she took her seat in front of Beth, things felt different. Normally she could feel the tension of sitting in front of the Snotty Twin Queen—an occasional poke or pop to her back, and Beth grinning innocently when she'd turn to look. But today, she might as well have been sitting in front of a busted balloon. No evil energy to block. No energy at all.

A quick glance showed her a Beth she'd never seen before. Swollen eyes with black rings. Pale skin. Lips puckered and cracked. Gena couldn't help but think the girl had cried so much she'd completely drained herself of all moisture. *Gross!*

"So say it," Beth whispered. "I know you're dying to."

Gena made a half turn. "Say what?"

"What you've wanted to say forever."

Gena glanced at Mr. Douglas sitting at his desk. "Are you trying to get me in trouble again? Because yesterday's detention was your fault."

Beth's breathing sounded uneven and worn. "I'm trying to get you to say what you've been thinking all this time. That I'm a stuck-up snob. A preppy snot nose. An ego in sneakers."

Gena grinned. "I've never thought those *exact* things, but they sum you up pretty good. I've always just thought you were a weenie."

"Good. We've cleared the air."

Gena was suddenly confused. Why would Beth want to clear the air with her? "We have?"

Beth shrugged. "I'm making a pros and cons list about moving to Dallas. Getting away from you is on the plus side."

"I hear the schools in Dallas are pretty big. Let's see, what are the odds of you being popular and making cheerleader?" Gena pretended to write some figures on a piece of paper.

"I'll be popular wherever I go." Beth snapped.

"And what happens if you're not? Afraid you'll be like . . . me?"

"Turn around before I get you in trouble again."

Gena started to turn around, then looked back. "I have just one more question. What did Juniper and I ever do to make you hate us?"

Beth opened her mouth to answer, but it was then that Mr. Douglas apologized for starting class late and began to teach.

★ ★ ★

Juniper didn't eat lunch in the cafeteria because she'd promised Mrs. Thompson, the librarian, she would help sort a box of donated books. She did pass through, leaning in and saying, "I've got it! We need to meet tonight."

"You've got what?" Gena asked as Juniper scooted off toward the library.

"The solution to your problem," Juniper called back. "It was in one of my books."

She disappeared around the corner and Gena looked at Anne. "Are you going to be there?"

"Not show up and miss the solution? You bet I'll be there!"

Gena nodded. She didn't know how much longer she could go without a reflection. She hoped Juniper really had something that would work.

★   ★   ★

When Gena got home, Rachael was in the kitchen whipping up another gourmet meal. "What are *you* doing here?"

Rachael grinned. "Cooking."

"Isn't it your night off?"

"Yep."

Gena didn't understand. This wasn't typical. "Don't you and Dad go out to eat on your night off?"

"Usually."

Gena waited. Nothing. "So . . . why are you cooking?"

Rachael shrugged. "I thought we'd all eat together tonight. Don't you like a little change once in a while?"

"Sure," she said, heading to her bedroom. *A little change? Lately the changes have been dumped on me like an avalanche.*

She watched TV for a little while, but her mind wasn't on the program. She kept wondering what solution Juniper had, and if it would really work. She finally couldn't take it anymore and reached for the phone.

"Sorry, Gena," Mrs. Lynch said. "Juniper's not home right now. She stayed after school for a Student Council meeting."

"Thanks," Gena said, clicking off the phone. She was ready to explode with curiosity.

It wasn't long before her dad came home and they all sat down to Rachael's dinner. Gena wished they'd gone out as usual. She would have preferred being alone when Juniper and Anne came over . . . just in case the solution called for something her dad might not like.

Rachael kept grinning through dinner. She and Dad exchanged bright glances, which told Gena they were sharing a secret. *Okay, okay, if you're about to get married or something then spill it! Just quit looking at each other like a couple of grinning possums.*

Finally Rachael spoke up. "Guess what?"

Gena looked up from the meal. "Are you asking me?"

"Yeah," Rachael said. "I've got some good news."

Gena held her breath. Good news to Rachael didn't necessarily mean good news to her.

"We've been invited to a grand ball!"

"Like Cinderella?" Gena asked.

"Yes!" Rachael exclaimed. "Aren't you excited?"

Gena looked over at her dad who was also beaming and happy. "Why should I be excited?" she asked. "I'm not going."

"Sure you are," Rachael said. "I sent the RSVP for three people."

Gena shrugged. "Fine. As long as I don't have to ride in a pumpkin."

"This is a special benefit ball for the hospital," Dad told her. "It's formal."

Ugh! Why me? "Are you telling me that I have to put on a fancy prom-type dress?"

"Yes," Rachael said, still giddy. "We're going tomorrow night to buy both of us gowns to wear. It's going to be so much fun."

For you. "I hate shopping. Can't I just tell you my size and you can grab something on sale?"

"Gena!" Dad's look said the rest.

"Okay, but not pink. I won't wear pink."

Rachael smiled even bigger. "We're going to have a ball of our own just shopping for dresses. I can't wait to see you try on some of those sequined gowns."

Gena nearly choked on her food. *Try on? As in the fitting room? With lots of mirrors? Juniper! Help!*

CHAPTER 6

The Banishing

"I didn't think you guys would ever get here!" Gena blurted as she let Juniper and Anne in the door. "I've got mucho mega-problems!"

"Yeah, and then there's the mirror thing," Anne added with a giggle.

Juniper laughed too. "Sorry," she said quickly when Gena gave her a stern look. "It was just a joke. No reflection on you."

Both girls howled with laughter as Gena pretended to push them back out the front door. "Come on. This is serious."

"Hello," Mr. Richmond said as he strolled into the living room. He spied the backpack Juniper was carrying. "You guys planning some important predictions tonight?"

Juniper looked back and shrugged.

"I figure that's got to be fortune telling stuff you've got in there. Gena wouldn't allow you to bring in school work. She knows if I caught her studying that I might have another heart attack." He winked and smiled, his face mellow.

Juniper smiled back. "It is fortune telling stuff. But we could go over the science vocabulary if that'd make you feel better."

"I already know the science words," Gena said. "Icky, pukey, gooey, gross, yucky, disgusting, putrid, and nauseating."

"We're studying the brain!" Anne said.

Gena rolled her eyes. "It never matters what we're studying in science, it all turns my stomach to a pretzel."

She motioned for them to follow her to her room. She was dying to get back there, but she didn't want to look suspicious in front of her dad. She shut the door and locked it as soon as they entered. "Okay, let's get started."

Juniper plopped down on the floor and unzipped the pack. "I can't believe I found this in one of my books. It's called a banishing. It's the perfect solution."

Anne dropped down by her and sat cross-legged. "Well, what is it?"

Gena approached more slowly. She wanted to get rid of Miss Pigtails, but the word *banishing* sounded a bit scary.

"Come over here," Juniper said, waving toward her. "You're the one who has to do this."

That's what Gena was afraid of. "And what's going to keep me from vanishing into the Twilight Zone?" she asked, squatting down.

Juniper gave her a look. "You're seeing someone else in your mirror, Gena. I'd say you're already in the T-Zone!"

She pulled out a mirror, some whipped cream in a spray can, four small silver candles, and a book of matches. "This is what you do. First, we'll dim the lights while you light the candles.

Then you'll lean forward and concentrate on the girl in the mirror." Juniper explained this intensely while placing a candle in each corner of the mirror that lay flat on the floor. "Then when you feel the time is right, you'll use this whip cream to draw an outline of the reflection you see." Juniper held the can up.

"Whipped cream?" Gena asked "Is that a proper tool of ancient spell-casters?"

Juniper sighed. "Do you really want to do this the old-fashioned way? That involved some sharp objects and blood."

"I'll stick to the whipped cream."

Juniper continued, "Once you've drawn the outline, visualize the girl drifting out of the mirror, and your own reflection taking her place." Juniper reached into her backpack and pulled out a small bottle of something that looked like dead fleas. "Then you'll sprinkle this on the reflection."

"What is it?" Anne asked.

"Pepper."

Gena grinned. "Wouldn't garlic be a better choice?"

"You're getting rid of a reflection, not a vampire," Juniper said.

Gena looked at the bottle of pepper. Coarse ground. No wonder it looked like fleas. "Are we going to sneeze her out?"

Juniper gave her a solid look, then shifted her eyes to Anne. "Pepper burns."

A chill caught Gena's arms and she shivered slightly. "This is getting intense. We're not going to hurt anyone, are we? Particularly . . . me?"

"Not as long as we stay focused." Juniper said. "Keep your concentration up. Both of you."

Anne nodded.

Juniper, looking stern again, added, "No matter what happens."

The chill returned, rolling down Gena's spine.

Juniper got up and turned off the light. "I hope no one disturbs us."

Gena took the matches and lit each candle. Her hand trembled, making it a harder task than usual. She didn't mind that Anne and Juniper saw her shake. They already knew she was a scaredy-cat.

As each candle lit, the mirror took on a life of its own, becoming a source of new light that flashed through the room. The flames danced slightly, inside and outside the mirror. The effect was dazzling.

"Concentrate," Juniper whispered.

Gena leaned forward just enough to see the reflection. Miss Pigtails was there, face glowing in the light of the candles' flames. She looked weak and drawn. Could the spell be working already?

Gena didn't take her eyes off her for a minute. The girl appeared to be staring back at her with her own intense concentration. Gena was careful not to flinch or look away. It was a stare-down.

Neither of them blinked. Gena didn't need to. It was hypnotic. She sat, fixed on the image of Miss Pigtails, concentrating on her own strength, and her ability to banish this reflection from her life forever. A few moments later, the reflection changed. Gena saw it, though she doubted Anne or Juniper did. The girl's eyes sagged in surrender. Gena took the whipped cream and sprayed it on the mirror. The first spurt shot out in a messy blob, spraying flecks of white everywhere. But she soon got control, and outlined the reflection just as Juniper had instructed her.

Without blinking, she picked up the pepper. Just before tilting it, she thought of a scary story she'd heard as a child about a woman who could shed her skin at night and put it back on the next morning. One night her husband poured pepper into her skin, and the next morning the woman screamed in agony as she burned to death. *Would Miss Pigtails scream in agony? Not if the mirror is protecting her,* Gena thought.

She sprinkled the pepper. It mostly bounced and rolled on the slick glass and got caught in the outline of whipped cream. *Uck!*

Gena waited. This was all the instructions she had. Finally Juniper spoke up.

"Pick up the mirror and take it to a bigger mirror."

Gena looked at her. "What?"

"Pick it up."

Anne narrowed her eyes and nodded as though to say, "Don't ask, just do it."

Gena picked up the mirror, careful not to drop it, and smear peppered whipped cream all over the carpet. She walked over to the mirror above her dresser.

"Now turn it facing the big mirror, and press it against it," Juniper said.

Gena thought that was about the silliest thing she'd ever heard, but Juniper was dead serious. She knew not to argue. Juniper had a sense about these things, no matter how silly.

She pressed the smaller mirror to the bigger mirror and held it there. "What happens now?"

Juniper let out a deep breath as she spoke. "You're reversing the process. This will get her out of your mirror. She'll be banished."

All three girls were crowded tightly around the large mirror. Gena pressed hard. The smaller mirror slid around because of the whipped cream.

"Hold it still," Juniper said.

Gena tried.

Juniper stepped back. "Now release it."

It took Gena a few seconds to get it unstuck, but she managed, then stood back next to Juniper. "What a mess!"

She still couldn't see her reflection, but that was because the mirror was coated in white goo with black freckles.

"Just wipe off the middle," Juniper said. "We have to know if it worked. Try to leave as much of the outline as possible."

Gena used her fingers. She managed to smear it even more. It looked like the fake frost that the stores put on their windows at Christmas. "Bleck!" She held out her hand and looked around for something to wipe it on. The floor was littered with dirty clothes. She grabbed the tee shirt she'd worn three days ago and wiped her hand. Then she used it to wipe the mirror. "I never liked this shirt much anyway." She wadded it into a ball, and tossed it back on the floor. As she turned around, she realized there was no use looking in the mirror. The looks on Juniper and Anne's faces were enough of a clue. Miss Pigtails was still there.

"It didn't work," Anne said.

Juniper looked more hopeful. "Give it time. Spells don't work in an instant. They have to reach the cosmos first and rearrange the settings."

"You make them sound like computer techies," Gena said.

Juniper shrugged. "When you look at life over-all, everything's like a huge computer program."

"More like a video game," Anne added.

"Yeah," Gena said. "And I'm losing big time!"

CHAPTER 7

A Big Fat No

It was late before Gena had a chance to sneak Twilight into her room. She curled up next to him on the bed and rubbed his ears. He snuggled close. The dark room made his eyes look an even color, but when her nightlight hit them just so, they flashed like tiny mirrors. *Like an animal caught in the headlights. Creepy.* Gena tried to close her own eyes and sleep. It seemed to take forever.

When she woke, her brain pounded like someone who'd just had a hard nap. Twilight was pawing at the litter in the cardboard box. She slid

53

out of bed and took care of her morning business, never getting near the dresser mirror. She wanted to be fully awake before looking. Her mind had to be alert to prepare herself for what might be reflected there. Would it still be Miss Pigtails or her typical early morning self—wild hair, sagging face, and droopy eyes? She definitely needed breakfast first.

After letting Twilight out for the day, she headed for the kitchen. Dad had already left for work. Some biscuits sat on a plate, along with some burnt bacon. *Why not?* She crunched and chewed. Sitting at the kitchen table, she wished there was a window she could look out. The world must be going in high speed by now. Everyone looking in mirrors, applying lipstick, brushing their hair, their teeth. *Wow. And people say they can't live without their televisions. Let them try existing without a mirror! Tough.* If she ever saw her reflection again, she'd look at herself in a whole new light. Gena removed some bacon rind from her mouth and thought about it some more. A word popped into her head—*perception*. She didn't know exactly what it meant, but she was sure it had something to do with how she was seen to herself and other people. She knew how the Snotty Twins saw her. And Juniper and Anne and Rachael and Dad. Or did she?

She scooted the chair back and stood up. *Stop thinking! Just do what you're avoiding!* She headed for the bathroom. Not wasting another moment, she rushed in and faced the mirror. *Aaaaargh!* The banishing hadn't worked. Miss Pigtails was still there, and she looked furious! For once her reflection matched Gena's mood.

Gena looked down at the sink. It was filled with splotches of shaving cream and Dad's whiskers. She picked up the can of shaving cream, thinking about the whipped cream outline she'd made the night before. Just for fun, she aimed the can at Miss Pigtails and outlined her again. Then she applied a mustache. And those fuzzy eyebrows had to go! She'd lathered her pretty good before realizing she'd better hurry for school. With any luck, Juniper was right. She had to hang on until the cosmos ticked in the right direction and the spell worked.

Surprisingly, she managed to make it to school about five minutes before the bell. Juniper and Anne were standing by the magnolia tree, chatting away. When Gena got closer, she nearly flipped. Nicole Hoffman was standing next to them. *Do I really want to do this?* Gena asked herself as she slowed her pace, strolling in their direction.

"Hi!" Juniper called, looking desperately happy to see her. Anne looked like she was trying to hold back some dynamite laughter.

Gena never got the chance to say hi. As she approached, she could hear Nicole blabbing away. "So . . . when are we going to get together to rehearse? I think we have a shot at winning first place in the duet category, but we really need to rehearse after school. Should my mom come pick you up tonight? We could practice at my house. We have lots of room to dance there. And I have some great ideas for the music. We are doing jazz, right? I'd rather do jazz instead of lyrical. Wouldn't you?"

Juniper shrugged and nodded and shrugged—like a mime who couldn't make up her mind whether to "walk against the wind" or do the "trapped in a box" routine. She finally spoke up and Gena was glad to hear another voice in the lopsided conversation. "Hang on, Nicole. Are you sure we really should be dance partners? Our styles are so different."

"True," Gena said. "Juniper actually manages to stay on her feet."

Nicole raised an eyebrow. "You just won't let me forget the Fourth-Grade Talent Show, will you? That wasn't my fault. The new taps on my shoes were slippery." She gave Gena a sugary grin. "We'll talk about it later, Juniper." She spun and headed off.

"What was that all about?" Gena asked.

Anne let out some giggles. "She's Juniper's new best friend."

Juniper shook her head. "I can't believe she's trying to use me to replace Beth."

They stood a moment before Juniper asked, "Well?"

Gena lowered her head. "It hasn't worked yet. Miss Pigtails is still in my mirror. Although this morning she got pied with a can full of shaving cream. I couldn't help myself. But it was fun."

"Give it time," Juniper said. "I'm sure it'll work."

"If it does, then maybe we can try it on Nicole," Gena teased, giving a sly grin.

"Don't I wish!" Juniper barely finished the sentence when the bell rang.

★ ★ ★

Beth sat up straight in her desk, looking perky and bright in a new outfit. Gena slipped in carefully, trying to be invisible. It didn't work.

"Have you heard the wonderful news?"

Gena held her breath. *Please don't tell me you're not moving after all.*

"Daddy has agreed to send me to a private school in Dallas. It will be much better than public school. You know, the kids are smarter . . . more activities. I'll be associating with better people. I mean, after all, they only take the best."

"The best? How'd you get in?"

"Cute. I'll try to remember my days at Avery with fondness." Beth turned up her pointy little nose with that statement.

"Which side of your brain will you use when remembering, the right or left? Oh wait, I forgot, yours is missing some pieces."

Beth gave her the famous "kiss my foot" look. "Blame it on the atmosphere around here." Then she shifted her hateful gaze toward Nicole.

Uh-oh! The Snotty Twins are on the outs. Gena watched Nicole doodling in her notebook. *If my reflection wasn't so messed up, this would be perfect!*

The rest of the day passed by as usual, except for the time Gena had to pee and couldn't go into the restroom until everyone else had cleared out. No matter how big the emergency, she couldn't risk anyone seeing her reflection in the mirrors.

She made it home, feeling tired and hungry. After grabbing a cupcake, she went to her room, dropped her backpack, and walked over to the bed. As she passed the mirror, something odd caught her eye. *What?* Miss Pigtails was there, but also this:

GET OUT OF MY MIRROR!

How weird! Gena had to get another mirror just to read what it said.

CHAPTER 8

The Ouija Speaks

"You've gotta get over here now!" Gena yelled into the phone. "And bring Anne." Gena couldn't believe it. She looked at the backward message again. *GET OUT OF MY MIRROR!* What did she write it with? Lipstick? Gena touched it with her finger. It was on the inside of the mirror. That's just great! And Miss Pigtails was staring out at her with a smirky grin.

It didn't take Juniper and Anne long to get there. They burst through the door like they were running away from a school bully, panting and heaving.

"What is it?" Juniper asked. "I'm guessing the banishing still hasn't worked."

"No, it hasn't," Gena said. "And now I know why that girl hogging my reflection always looks so ticked off."

She led them back to her bedroom. One look at the mirror and their faces dropped in shock.

"What does this mean?" Anne asked.

Gena handed her the smaller mirror to read it. "It looks as though I'm not the only one who's lost her reflection."

Juniper stood, looking dazed. "Wow."

"Is that all you can say?" Gena paced around, hoping one of them had a solution for this. "What am I going to do? What if Rachael comes in here to pick up my dirty clothes and sees this writing? What's going on?"

Anne just shrugged. Juniper looked at Gena. "Is this message only in this mirror?"

"I don't know. I haven't checked the others."

Anne handed her the small mirror. Gena looked in. There it was. "How did I miss this before? It's going to be in every mirror I look into now!"

"At least it's covering some of the reflection," Anne offered. "You didn't want to see all of her anyway, did you?"

"I don't want to see any of her!"

Juniper turned, stroking her neck and deep in thought. "That's why the banishing didn't work."

"Why?" Gena asked.

"Because it's not that she's overtaken your reflection. You've swapped reflections . . . "

"And?" Gena wished Juniper would get to the point.

Juniper nodded, knowingly. "We should have done a reversal, not a banishing."

"Great," Gena sputtered. "Do I have to mix up some more whipped cream and pepper? Because frankly, that kinda made me nauseated."

"As nauseated as this reflection makes you?" Anne asked.

"Errrrrrrgh." Groaning was the only answer she could think of at the moment.

Anne looked perky and alert. "So, are we going to do a reversal?"

Anne lives for this stuff. "I've got a better idea," Gena said. "Why don't we find out who this girl is?"

"She's got a point," Juniper said to Anne.

Meeeeow! Gena felt Twilight's fur slink against her leg. She picked him up and cuddled him. "And here's another mystery we can solve," she said.

"Why that cat has two bizarre-looking eyes that don't match?" Juniper asked.

"Don't listen to Juniper," Gena said to Twilight in baby talk. "I think you have pretty eyes."

Juniper giggled. "Pretty if you're a cat from some distant alien planet!"

"Stop it! You're going to hurt his feelings."

"Listen, I've got dance tonight, and I need to solve my own problem of how to keep Nicole away from me. I think we should go ahead and do what we need to do."

Anne leaned toward them. "And what is it we need to do . . . exactly?"

Juniper shrugged. "I don't have the info for doing a reversal right now. I'll have to look that up at home. But we can still try and find out who she is."

Gena looked at Miss Pigtails. "Let's do it quick!"

Gena brought out the fancy Ouija board that Rachael had once given her as a peace offering. They sat around it and placed their fingers on the crystal planchette.

"Oh no," Gena said, turning her face away.

Anne looked alarmed. "What's wrong?"

"I can see her reflection in the pointer."

Juniper scooted in closer. "Try to lean back so you can't see it."

Gena did. Leaning back and keeping her fingers steady would take some major talent and lots of concentration. Oh well, she needed concentration for the Ouija anyway.

"Who's going to ask the questions?"

"It's your ordeal," Juniper said.

Gena closed her eyes and formulated a question. She asked it slowly so the cosmos wouldn't mistake it for one of her FAQs like *How can I keep Dad from seeing my test grade?* Or *What did I ever do to deserve living in the same town as the Snotty Twins?* Her urgent question came out, "Who is the girl in my mirror?"

The planchette sat as still as a rock for a few moments. Gena wondered if it would move. Finally, it jerked and slid slightly. Then it spelled T-A-Y (pause) L-O-R.

"Taylor! Her name is Taylor." Anne said, exploding with excitement.

Juniper blew on her fingertips and put them back on the planchette. "Calm down. We don't want to scare off the vibes."

Anne scooched forward and crossed her legs in a different position.

Gena, sensing they were ready, asked another question. "Why is she in my mirror?"

The Ouija didn't waste any time with an answer. "T-R-A-N-S-I-E-N-T.

"What does that spell?" Anne asked.

Gena dove for her backpack and pulled out some paper and a pen. She wrote it out. Transient. "Hmmm . . . I must have been absent the day we studied this one. You're the honor student, Juniper. What does it spell?"

Juniper shrugged. So did Anne.

"Aaaargh! I'll go into Dad's office and grab a dictionary." She rushed down the hall with Twilight tagging along at her heels. It occurred to her again that she hadn't let the cat inside. And he hadn't snuck in when Juniper and Anne had arrived. But she had more important things to worry about at the moment. She'd solve the magically appearing kitty mystery after she'd solved this one. She grabbed her Dad's *Oxford Desk Dictionary* and ran back.

Squatting on her knees, she flipped through. There were a lot of words under the letter *T*. Why was that? She finally found it. "It's a real word. *Transient* . . . of short duration; passing. Temporary visitor, worker, etc. Transitory, temporary, fleeting, ephemeral, short-lived, short term."

"Well, that's good," Anne said.

Gena clapped the dictionary closed. "How?"

"Short-lived. Short-term. Temporary. Sounds like she'll go away on her own soon."

Gena felt hopeful. "You think?"

Juniper nodded. "Let's hope that's right. Give it a few more days. If you're not seeing yourself by this weekend. We'll do a reversal."

Suddenly Gena's hopefulness sagged. "You guys, I have to go shopping with Rachael. She wants me to try on dresses. What am I going to do?"

Juniper and Anne looked at each other. Gena wondered if they were concerned about her problem or just shocked that she'd actually try on a dress.

"Just try to think short-term," Juniper said, standing up to go.

"Yeah," Anne agreed, standing up too. "The Ouija wouldn't lie."

"Great," Gena moaned. "In the meantime I'll have to put up with Taylor the Transient. Could my life get any better than this?"

Meow. Twilight stepped onto her lap and rubbed his head on her chin.

CHAPTER 9

A Shopping We Will Go

*S*hort-lived. Short-term. Temporary. How short-term? Gena wondered as she slipped into the passenger side of Rachael's Volkswagen Beetle and buckled up. *Could this suddenly go away at any minute? Any second? Poof! I'd look in the mirror and say, "I'm ba-ack!"* Once the car was rolling, she scrunched down to relax. That's when she glanced toward the window and saw Miss Pigtails reflected in the side-view mirror. *Great!* She sat up again. She was pretty sure all Rachael could see were the cars approaching in the right lane, but she didn't want to take any chances.

"Are you excited?" Rachael asked, her voice bubbly like a kid's.

"About buying a dress? You're joking, right?"

Rachael's dimples disappeared. "I'm excited. I thought we'd do the whole girl thing. Buy our dresses, have ice cream, maybe even go to a movie. This is *our* night."

Gena drummed her fingers on the armrest. "We'll probably spend the whole time just looking for a dress for me. I'm not easy to please when it comes to girly things."

"Don't worry," Rachael said, dimples returning. "You've never shopped with me before."

It wasn't long before Rachael was pulling into a parking spot outside the mall. The mall. The humongous . . . shiny . . . mirrored mall! Gena slumped down, but when she saw the reflection in the side mirror again, she shot back up. Her mind raced. How was she going to make it inside without Rachael seeing the distorted reflection in every mirrored panel on the mall? Then she noticed the cinema entrance sticking out from the rest of the building. It was a beautiful gray brick! "Let's cut through there."

"But the department store I like is right here where I parked," Rachael said.

"What if we do decide to see a movie? Wouldn't it make more sense to go through there and see what time it starts? I hate missing the previews at the beginning. That's my favorite part. Let's go."

She didn't give Rachael time to argue. She jumped out of the car and wormed through the middle of the parking lot toward the cinema. Rachael trotted to keep up.

"At this pace I may be too tired to see a movie," Rachael said.

Gena ignored her and kept going. Soon they were inside and on the fancy carpet in front of the ticket booth. Gena kept walking out into the mall, not thinking about anything but getting to the department store without Rachael seeing Miss Pigtails in a plate-glass window.

"Hey!" Rachael called, running up and pulling Gena to a stop. "Aren't you forgetting something?"

Gena shrugged. *Please don't let this be one of those stupid grown-up lesson I'm supposed to learn.*

"You forgot to stop to see what time the movie started.

Gena felt like a real dummy. *Don't blow it, Richmond. You can get through this.*

She walked back onto the carpet and looked at the marquee. "I don't know. I really don't see anything that I'd want to waste two hours of my life on. How about you?"

Rachael sighed. "Let's just go buy the dress."

They made it down the mall, inside the store, and up the escalator. "What size do you wear?" Rachael asked.

"In dresses? I have no clue. In tee shirts, big and baggy."

Rachael laughed. "No kidding. You always look like you're wearing Robert's tee shirts."

Gena looked down at her dad's shirt, hanging to her knees. "I am."

Rachael led her to the teen section. "We'll start here."

There were two full racks of formal gowns, most marked on sale. "Isn't this the prom dresses?"

"If you're buying them for a prom," Rachael said. "They are also called formals. Remember this ball is formal." She immediately reached for a pale-green satin dress and held it up.

Gena shrugged. "Well, at least it's not pink."

Rachael took one that was the same style in royal blue, and a calf-length dress in a dark burgundy. "Shall we start with these?"

"I can't talk you into sewing a ruffle around one of Dad's tee shirts?" Gena asked.

Rachael's answer was a "get serious!" look.

"Okay, but don't follow me into the dressing room. I'm shy."

"What?" Rachael followed.

"Really. I don't like people watching me change clothes."

"We're both girls," Rachael said. "And what about gym class?"

"That's the beauty of wearing Dad's shirts. They're also like wearing a tent. I just slip my gym shorts on underneath."

Rachael shook her head. "You are as odd as your father."

Gena grinned as she took the dresses from Rachael's hand. "That's why you love us."

She headed into the dressing room and closed the door. Three mirrors! *Give me a break!* Looking down at the floor, she decided to try on the green dress first. She'd never admit this to a single living soul, but she did think they were sort of pretty. She had a tugging match with the back zipper, but the dress really seemed to fit. She looked in the mirror. *How long is short-term?* Miss Pigtails stood full-length in her plaid skirt and white buttoned blouse. Her face was hidden behind the smeared backward sentence of lipstick. Gena sighed. She really wanted to see herself. Really.

She stepped out of the stall and walked out to where Rachael was browsing through the costume jewelry. "What'd ya think?"

Rachael's face melted into an expression of awe. "Gena, that color is perfect on you!" She stepped up and grabbed a handful of Gena's hair, twisted it and brought it up to rest on top of her head. "And when we get your hair done . . . "

"Hang on!" Gena stepped back, shaking her hair loose. "You never said anything about hairdos."

Rachael held up her hands in surrender. "Fine. The dress is lovely."

Gena looked down, trying to see as much of the dress as she could.

"Do you want to try on the others?" Rachael asked.

Gena did like this color. A lot. "Nah. If you think this one is *lovely,* then it works for me." She wondered how Anne would react if she saw it. This was just the type of dress Anne would flip over.

Gena went back into the dressing room to change. Before heading out, she took off her sneaker and threw it at the reflection. Miss Pigtails actually winced. *Creepy.* Gena grabbed her shoe and rushed away, feeling weirded-out.

CHAPTER 10

Tea Time

Gena steered Rachael away from the ice cream shop when she remembered the mirrored-tile walls inside. She lured her back to the movies instead. Although Rachael was wanting to see the latest blockbuster, Gena talked her into seeing a horror flick. Rachael didn't exactly see it because she squelched in her seat, keeping her face buried in her hands. Gena didn't exactly see it either. Her mind was on Taylor the Transient, a.k.a. Miss Pigtails. And besides, Gena had already seen the movie three times.

Once the Rachael/Gena bonding time ended, Rachael dropped Gena off at Juniper's house.

"Well, that was fun," Rachael said.

Gena shrugged. "Yeah. Thanks for the dress."

Rachael smiled as Gena stepped out of the car.

"Hi, Gena!" Mrs. Lynch said through a pleasant smile. She waved at Rachael backing the Beetle out of the driveway. "Juniper is in her room. You can go on back."

"Actually, Ms. Joy, I came to see you."

Joy Lynch gave her a twisted expression. "Me?"

Gena shuffled her feet. "Could you read my tea leaves?"

The smile returned. "Of course! Come on, I'll boil some water. Juniper!"

Juniper came bouncing in. "Hey."

"Hey," Gena answered quietly.

Juniper stood for a moment then asked. "How was shopping?"

Gena heaved a major sigh. "A lot of work! That whole place is a looking glass."

"No change?" Juniper asked.

Gena shook her head.

"Come on, girls," Mrs. Lynch called. "Gena, this is going to be strong tea. I have to have plenty of leaves left on the bottom of the cup."

It seemed forever before the tea was ready and cool enough to drink.

"I would ask what you've been up to lately," Mrs. Lynch said, "but I can't. I don't want any prior information to upset the reading."

Gena sipped slowly. Ugh! She wasn't kidding when she said strong. "Brisk," she said, trying not to show a sour face.

Joy Lynch laughed. "Now you know why people prefer tarot readers."

After Gena gagged down the last sip, she swirled the remaining goop at the bottom of the cup, and handed it to Juniper's mom.

Mrs. Lynch studied the cup with an intense look. "Gena. What's this business with your father?"

Gena shrugged. "I don't know." She didn't. She didn't want to know. *Just get on with the business about me.*

Mrs. Lynch twitched her mouth back and forth. Gena assumed it was another sign of concentration.

She raised an eyebrow and looked up. "Gena, when did you get a pet?"

Gena flinched, guilt and shock tunneling through her. *Boy, Juniper's mom is good!* "I don't have a pet."

"According to this you do."

Gena looked over at Juniper, sitting next to her mom at the kitchen table. Her look was a giveaway too. "Come on, Mom. Her apartment doesn't allow pets."

Thanks Juniper!

Mrs. Lynch grinned. "Never mind. We'll forget your secret pet for now. But that rascal is about to stir up something. I can't tell exactly what the trouble will be, but if it's you getting caught, your dad may have to pay a hefty fine. Or worse. I would hate for you to get evicted."

Gena squirmed. *Oh, brother!* "Do you see us getting evicted?"

"No," she said quietly.

Gena relaxed a bit.

"You're not here for the fun of it, are you?" Mrs. Lynch asked.

"You tell me," Gena said, pointing at the saggy tea leaves, now drying on the cup.

"You just don't seem yourself. At least, according to the reading."

Gena nodded. "You might say that."

Mrs. Lynch kept staring into the cup. "Have you taken a good hard look at yourself lately?"

Juniper turned her head, trying to conceal a giggle.

Gena didn't find it funny. "That's the problem. I can't see myself."

Mrs. Lynch gave Gena a grave look. "Sweetheart, you've got to evaluate things. Sort your priorities. Consider what's yours and isn't yours. Not everything is obvious. Not all of your possessions belong to you. Things aren't always as they appear. Understand?"

"Not a word," Gena said. It seemed like a lot of double-talk to her. "Just answer this. Will it get better . . . soon?"

Mrs. Lynch didn't look down. She kept her eyes focused on Gena. "If you let it. Look in the obvious places. Sometimes the smallest movement can cause an earthquake. If something is different, you brought about that change. Think about it."

She didn't give Gena or Juniper a chance to say anything else. She took the cup to the sink and tossed the tea leaves into the garbage disposal, then ran the water.

★ ★ ★

"So I drank that nasty crap for nothing?" Gena asked, back in Juniper's room.

"Not necessarily," Juniper answered. "We can think about what Mom said. You'd be surprised how many times I have to decode what she tells me. By the way, did you get a dress?"

Gena didn't want to make a big deal about it. Especially not to Juniper. "Yeah, and it's pukey green." She wanted to change the subject quick.

"What about the reversal? Did you look that up?"

"Yes, but you aren't going to like it."

Eek.

Both girls jumped at the noise. "What was that?" Gena whispered. She looked around Juniper's room. It was a fortune telling museum. Her heart pounded.

"Shhh," Juniper mouthed, her finger on her lips. "I'll get that information right now," she said, talking kind of phony. She tiptoed over to her bed and in a flash pulled up the bedcovers hanging to the floor. "Jonathan, get your skinny butt out from under there!"

Juniper's brother, Jonathan, shot out in a hurry and stood by the bedroom door, wiggling his behind and chanting, "Gena bought a dress! Gena bought a dress!"

"Yeah, and I'm gonna make you wear it if you don't get out of here!" Gena yelled.

Juniper ran toward him, "Get out!"

Jonathan slipped through the door and slammed it shut.

"That little creep," Juniper said, locking the door. "Now you know why I'd rather meet at your apartment."

Gena took a few deep breaths to steady herself. "About that reversal."

"Like I said," Juniper repeated, "You aren't going to like it."

CHAPTER 11

The Eyes Have It

Mrs. Lynch drove Gena home. Juniper stuck her head out of the car window as Gena headed toward her apartment. "Think about it!"

Gena nodded. She'd think about it all right. She'd think long and hard about how impossible it would be! Juniper's reversal idea was a trick that even Houdini couldn't pull off.

She slipped inside, careful not to wake her dad who was snoozing in a recliner with the remote control resting in his lap. When she got to her bedroom, she saw the new dress, still concealed in a plastic bag, hanging on the inside of the door. She lifted the plastic to admire it again. *Get a grip, Richmond!* She pulled the bag back down and hung the dress over the dresser mirror to hide Miss Pigtails from view. As she turned around, she tripped over something stout. *Rrr-aoerrrr!* "Twilight! How on earth did you get in here!"

Gena picked him up and they settled on the bed. Her thoughts strayed from the reversal spell to her mysterious new cat. *Dad has to know? Or maybe Rachael? One of them is letting this cat in.* But Dad would have a thousand conniptions if he knew. And Rachael? Surely she'd say something— like giving a lecture about putting everyone at risk by breaking the rules and chancing us getting the boot. And knowing Rachael, she'd promise not to tell Dad in return for keeping Twilight out of the apartment. It just didn't make sense.

Gena checked her room for holes in the wall. None that a big cat like Twilight could fit through. She did notice the odor of pesticide. Ah ha! The exterminator had been in for the monthly spray job. He could have let Twilight in.

Gena's sank down onto her bed. She had to get things back to normal. This was just not her typical existence. She grabbed a notepad.

1.) New cat

2.) No reflection

3.) Arch-enemy is moving away (the only good part)

4.) I have to wear a fancy dress to a ball

She laughed when she looked at the list. Maybe she could be on a new TV show called *Whose Life Is It Anyway?* 'cause this was certainly not hers!

She picked up the phone. "Juniper? Explain that reversal to me again."

She heard Juniper sigh over the phone. Then a moment of dead air separated them. "Juniper?"

"Hang on. I have to go get the book."

She could hear Juniper's breath on the other end, and figured she was reading the reversal over again.

Finally, "Okay, here goes. Now remember, we're making it simple."

"Yeah, simple for you!" Gena reminded her.

"Just listen," Juniper said. "You'll have to put on a white button blouse and a plaid skirt."

Gena saw it in her mind. Just imagining it was embarrassing! "Are you sure that's important?"

"Only if you want your reflection back. Then you'll have to put your hair in braids."

"Will I have to get an eyebrow pencil and draw that caterpillar across my forehead? I mean, I am supposed to look just like her, right?"

Juniper giggled at that. "I think you can pass on the bushy eyebrows. Then you'll have to stand in front of the mirror and say this chant, 'Magic mirror, mighty mirror, listen to my plea. Send this girl her own true self, and my image back to me. Like lost souls caught in the dark, our reflections we can't see. So send this girl her reflection back, and return mine to me.'"

Gena snorted a laugh. "I didn't like it when you read it at your house, and I still don't like it."

"I told you so," Juniper said. "Just think about it. Desperate times call for desperate measures."

"I'm just not so sure I'm that desperate! And where on earth am I going to get a white shirt and plaid skirt? Certainly not in the stores I went into this afternoon with Rachael."

"I'm sure you can find them at a thrift store or something," Juniper said. "Why don't we wait and talk to Anne about this? She may have a better way to do it. And remember, we'd be right there, cheering you on."

"Oh no! No way! I wouldn't do this in front of anyone in the world. Not even my best friends."

"You'll be doing it in front of that girl in the mirror," Juniper reminded her. "Didn't you say she ducked when you chucked your shoe at her? She must be able to see you."

Gena glanced over at the mirror, now mostly blocked by the dress. Could Miss Pigtails see her? Was it like actually seeing through the looking glass? And if she could see through, could she step through? Twilight rubbed against Gena's leg and gave her a shivery chill. How did Twilight get in again?

"Gena? Are you there?"

Gena was too spooked to speak.

"Gena? Talk to me."

Gena found her voice. "I'll call you tomorrow. I think I should give this some thought. And you're right. We'll ask Anne. Good night."

She hung up the phone before hearing Juniper say "Bye." She went to the dresser and pushed the dress to one side, and slowly peeked around. Miss Pigtails peeked back. Gena touched the mirror. Solid. For some reason she was sure her hand would sink right into it like it was made of water. She pressed it in several places. Hard as a rock. The girl's reflection did just as Gena, pressing her side of the mirror too. Gena couldn't tell if it was in perfect synchronization or if the girl had decided to test her side also. She let go of the dress and let it slip back over the mirror. She was way too scared to turn the light out for bed. She just slipped under the covers with it on. Twilight curled up at her chin.

She tilted her head and looked at the cat. Those eyes. Those twilight eyes. Then Gena noticed something that sent her flying up off the bed.

"No way!" She took the startled cat in her arms and looked into his right eye. It was as glassy as a mirror, and reflected there . . . was her! "I can see myself in your eyes."

She turned his head and looked into his left eye. "No!" She was Miss Pigtails in that one. She tilted his head back the other way. She was still there, reflected in his blue eye. "It's me! It's me!" She tried to do a dance, but Twilight jumped from her arms and strolled over to the corner. He settled on a pile of dirty clothes she'd kicked there to make room for some other things. Gena fell back on the bed, smiling. "It's really me!"

CHAPTER 12

Disappearing Act

Gena woke to the smell of cinnamon seeping under the door and filling the room. She stretched, yawned, and looked at the clock. 10:12 a.m., typical waking time for a Saturday. And to add to this great day, she'd be able to see herself in Twilight's eye. That beautiful blue eye! It was about time she was able to check herself out . . . just to make sure the part in her hair was straight, or that she didn't have anything green and moldy-looking sticking to her front teeth.

"Kitty, kitty, kitty," she called softly. The room felt empty. She sat up and looked toward the corner. The pile of dirty clothes were only that—a pile of dirty clothes. No Twilight. Gena began her short search.

She checked in the closet . . . under the bed . . . under the dresser. That was it. There was no place else for a cat to hide. The door was shut tight and locked. He couldn't have gotten out that way. She pulled out the litter box. It hadn't been touched.

She checked behind the dress, and saw Miss Pigtails smiling back. Suddenly the smell of cinnamon was the only cheery thing about this Saturday. Hiding any evidence of Twilight, she went into the kitchen for her breakfast. Dad had made cinnamon toast, which she normally scarfed down, but today her mind wasn't on her taste buds.

Would she need to find a plaid skirt and white blouse? *Aaargh! No!*

She grabbed the phone and punched the numbers with desperation. She couldn't count on

Twilight. He came and went mysteriously like a transient. Gena patted her foot while the phone rang over and over.

She was about to give up when a voice came on the line. "Hullo?"

"Jonathan, I have to talk to Juniper."

"Why?"

"None of your business, nosey, now put her on the phone!"

"What'll you give me?"

Gena was losing patience fast. "A black eye if you don't get her."

"Are you going to beat me up with your *dress* on?" He barked with laughter, making Gena all the more infuriated.

"How does Juniper put up with you? Get her now!"

"Gena's got a dre-ess! Gena's got a dre-ess!"

She banged the phone against the kitchen table. "Hear that? Next time it will be your head. Now tell you sister to come to the phone."

"I can't."

Gena swallowed an urge to scream. "Why?"

"Because she's not here."

Sigh. "Why didn't you say so in the first place?"

She heard him snicker through his nose. "Because you didn't ask."

"Jonathan, please listen and try to explain like a human instead of like the alien matter from Planet Doofus that you really are. Where is Juniper?"

"She went to Nicole's house."

Gena wasn't expecting that. His words twisted her thoughts. "Are you sure she didn't go to Anne's?"

"She went to Nicole's to practice some stupid dance."

"Whatever," Gena said, clicking off the phone. *Nicole's? Guess Juniper finally gave in.*

She dialed Anne's house.

"Hello?"

"Thank goodness, you're home!" Gena blurted. "Please tell me I won't have to ever wear a plaid skirt."

Anne laughed. "Am I missing something?"

"Never mind. We need to have a meeting of the Fortune Tellers Club ASAP."

"Sure," Anne said. "I could come over right now."

"Not now, we have to wait for Juniper to get back from Nicole's."

"Nicole's?"

"Don't ask," Gena said. "Let's plan it for this afternoon."

She heard Anne shuffling on the other end of the line. "Just give me a call once you've set it up with Juniper."

"Sure." Gena hung up the phone, feeling like a mouse in a maze. She thought about Twilight and his two-colored eyes. Why did Miss Pigtails reflect on one side and her on the other? That cat was a key. A major key! Could he hold the secret to a reversal, one that could be done with dignity?

She threw on some clothes and went searching for him outside. She had to be careful not to look as though she was searching for an animal. The apartment manager was always roaming the grounds on a golf cart, especially on Saturdays. Gena strolled about as though she was just bored or taking in some fresh air, but she managed to check every laundry room, balcony, and storm drain, just in case he was lounging about. She even looked up at the roof. *Three stories up? Impossible.*

After thirty minutes of hide and seek, Gena decided that Twilight was not on the grounds.

When she got back to the apartment, the light was blinking on the answering machine. She pressed the button. Juniper's voice, sounding distant and robotic said, "Did you think about it yet?" *Beep!*

She grabbed the phone and dialed. *If that twerpy Jonathan answers . . .* "Juniper! You're home."

"Yeah." Juniper sounded winded and tired. "Nicole and I were practicing our duet."

"I need you and Anne to get over here right away. It's a matter of life and death."

"Good," Juniper said. "Nicole asked me to go skating with her this afternoon, but I told her I already had plans with you. At least now I'm not a liar."

"Doesn't she reserve Saturday afternoons for hanging out at the mall with Beth? Remember, that's why we never go to the mall on Saturday afternoon?"

Juniper laughed. "Beth's about to go bye-bye, and she's about to be stuck without a mall buddy."

"Well, I need you and Anne over here so I won't always be stuck without my reflection. I've made a new discovery that just might help the reversal."

"Will it work?" Juniper asked.

Gena closed her eyes and took a deep breath. "It better," she said. "'Cause my life is in the toilet right now, and I want out before someone flushes."

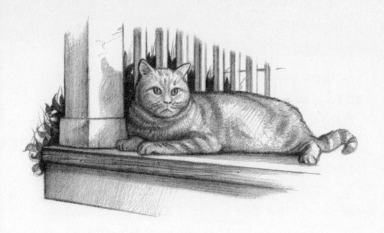

CHAPTER 13

Cat-Napper

"That's impossible," Anne said, shaking her head.

"So is losing your reflection," Gena reminded her.

The girls sat in a circle on the floor, soaking in the information about Twilight.

"Don't you get it?" Gena said. "Twilight is a key. If I can see my reflection in one of his eyes and that girl in the other, then he has to be a major solution to this problem."

Juniper nodded. "Let's get him and see if we can't figure something out."

Gena sagged. "I wish it was that easy. I can't find him. I've looked all over the apartment complex. He's vanished."

"Cats roam all over the place, Gena," Anne said. "He's probably not in the complex. Maybe we should search for him on the other streets."

Juniper stood up. "No maybes about it, let's go."

They hopped on their bikes and glided out the front gates. Taking a right, Gena pedaled ahead just a bit, and focused her thoughts. *If I were a cat, where would I go?* She saw Twilight in her mind's eye, and her own reflection blinking back at her. Somehow she felt that visualizing him would psychically lead her on. He had to be prowling close by. She heard that cats were nocturnal, staying awake at night and sleeping in the day, but this couldn't be true for Twilight. He slept in her room at night. Or did he? He was there when she went to sleep, and up until this morning, he was there when she woke up. But he did have that mysterious way of coming and going. She couldn't be sure about that, but she could be sure that doubting was not helping her to concentrate. Turning her bike left onto the next street, she kept going, glancing in yards and trees for her cat.

At the stop sign, the girls looked at each other. "No cats on that road," Anne said.

Gena shrugged. "Okay, let's go." She led them through a private alley that served as a back drive-way for the houses on the street they'd just left.

"I get it!" Juniper called. "An alley cat!"

Gena didn't laugh. She hadn't intended it to be a joke. She did see one fat fluffy cat curled up on the hood of a car. Not Twilight. Not even close! This cat was solid white, probably with some goofy name like Fluffy or Snowball. She looked back over her shoulder. Juniper and Anne were pedaling at a medium pace, their eyes darting back and forth in the search.

They came out onto a bigger street that ran down by the Dairy Treat. Gena didn't want to stop, but Juniper zoomed ahead and motioned them into the parking lot. "I didn't eat lunch today. Let's stop so I can at least fuel up on some fries."

Sitting in the booth, Gena saw a bulletin board. She sipped her Coke. "Maybe I should put up a notice."

"For the cat or your reflection?" Anne asked.

Gena grinned. "The cat, dummy."

"And say what?" Juniper sputtered, her mouth full of French fry mush. "Please return him to me at the Royal Court Apartments. You can't miss it, it has the *No Pets Allowed* sign out front."

"I could give your address or Anne's." She couldn't resist scrunching her nose in a "Na Na Na Na Na Na" fashion.

"Or we could just keep searching," Anne said. That's what they did.

They headed down Main Street, checking every parking lot and storefront. They rode around to the back of one small shopping center, only to be blocked by a large delivery truck.

The afternoon was sunny, but the breeze was mild, and it stirred thoughts in Gena of her dad pushing her on a swing when she was small. She remembered the fun times at the park. The teeter-totter. The slide. The sandbox . . . She skidded her bike and made a sharp U-turn.

"What?" Juniper said, hitting her brakes.

"Remember the park?" Gena asked.

Both girls nodded.

"My dad used to keep an eye on me when I played in the sandbox because it attracted stray cats who pottied in it."

Anne shivered dramatically. "Gross!"

Gena smiled. "Maybe he's at the park."

"It's worth a try," Juniper said. They turned and followed Gena.

The park was crowded with small children, and the smell of grilled hotdogs. The sandbox was full of kids, packing sand in plastic pails and bowls.

"No cats here," Anne said.

Gena had already realized that. Her heart sank little by little with each dead end. If she didn't find Twilight soon, it would be thumping in her toes.

"Anymore suggestions?" Juniper asked.

Gena nodded toward the neighborhood behind the Catholic church. "Let's look there."

With a sigh, Juniper settled back on her bike. So did Anne. They cut through the church parking lot, and bumped off the curb. That's when Gena saw him. Curled up and cozy on the porch of a large house.

"Twilight!" She dropped her bike and bounced up the steps to where he was. *Meow.* She picked him up and cuddled him close. "You naughty kitty. You should stay close to the apartments. You could get hurt."

"What are doing with my cat?"

Gena whipped around to face a girl standing in the doorway. Stunned into silence, her mouth dropped.

So did the girl's. "It's you!" she screamed. "You're the ugly girl I can't get out of my mirror!"

That snapped Gena back to reality. "I'm ugly? At least I have two eyebrows and enough sense not to wear pigtails."

The girl stepped out, hands planted firmly on her waist. "I want you off my porch and out of my mirror!"

"You think I want you in mine? Get real! And I'll be happy to get off your stupid porch." She started down the steps, although she really wanted to yank those pigtails and scream until she was hoarse.

"And put down my cat!" the girl yelled.

"Your cat? He sleeps at my apartment. He's mine."

"Are you nuts?" the girl said, walking down toward Gena. "I've had Hobo for three years."

"Hobo? What a dumb name for a cat. His name is Twilight."

"Now that's dumb," the girl said, reaching for him.

Gena tucked him under her arm and turned to run. The girl ran behind her, snatching at the cat. They passed Juniper and Anne, both straddling their bikes and taking in the scene.

"You can't steal my cat," the girl argued, grabbing and pulling him.

"You're going to hurt him," Gena said, tugging back.

"You threw a shoe at me!"

"You messed up my mirror with lipstick!"

Juniper rushed over and eased Twilight away. "Taylor."

The girl looked at Juniper, then back at Gena, then Juniper. "How'd you know my name?"

"I'm Juniper. This is Anne, and you're fighting with Gena."

Taylor took Twilight from Juniper and stroked his back. "I promise you he's my cat."

"I believe you," Juniper said.

Gena's sinking heart dropped like a rock. "Why are you siding with her?"

"Don't you get it?" Juniper said. "The cat isn't the solution. He's the problem. I bet he's the reason you see each other in the mirror."

Anne nodded. "I think Juniper's right."

Gena watched as Taylor rubbed her pudgy nose against Twilight's ear. "Then how do we solve it?"

"Give him up," Juniper said. "You can't have a cat in your apartment anyway. Just let him go. I bet once he's out of your life, you'll be seeing yourself again."

Gena hated the thought. A hot rush built up inside her. She wanted to lash out at everybody and everything. She swallowed the feeling like a lump of hot coal. "How can you be sure?"

Juniper looked her in the eyes. "I've got a tingling. And it's never wrong."

Anne reached over to pet Twilight, but Taylor back away. "How come we don't know you?" Anne asked. "Don't you go to Avery Middle School?"

"No," Taylor said. "I go there, to St. Laurence Catholic School."

Juniper smiled. "That explains the plaid skirt."

St. Laurence Catholic School. A private school. Gena thought of Beth going to a private school in Dallas. Would she have to wear a uniform too? She snapped back to reality and walked over to her bike. "I don't argue with Juniper's tinglings." And leaving the other girls behind, she sped off for home.

CHAPTER 14

The Ball

Juniper had been right. Gena saw her own reflection in her dresser mirror, and she suddenly felt light as a feather. But she still drudged about, getting rid of the cat food, litter, and other items she'd hidden. Even though she'd only owned Twilight part-time, she had an empty space in her heart. She missed his fluffed fur, gray nose, and odd eyes. *Oh well,* she thought. *It was only a matter of time before I got us kicked out of the apartment.*

The doorbell rang. "Thanks for leaving us there," Anne said, sashaying in. Juniper followed.

"Sorry," Gena said, quietly. "I just couldn't think straight."

Anne smiled as though she'd only been kidding. "So, are you seeing yourself?"

"Yep," Gena said, forcing a smile back.

"And it happened without dressing you up in a Catholic school girl uniform!" Juniper teased.

"Amen to that," Gena said. It took a minute for the girls to catch on, then they giggled.

Anne's face lit up. "Speaking of clothes, you never showed us your new dress!"

"And I never will. I plan to sneak in and out of that ball next Saturday, and then donate the dress to some desperate prom queen."

"Desperate?" Juniper said. "Like Nicole? She's going to drive me nuts trying to be my new best friend."

"Or is it the other way around?" Gena asked.

"Anyway," Juniper continued. "We're going to a special ballet production together tonight. Her mom had already bought tickets, and my mom thought it would be impolite to say no. Help!"

"How about a banishing?" Gena suggested. "But what would you wear for that?"

They giggled. "Anyway, I've got to get going so I can get ready."

"Yeah, I gotta go too," Anne said.

Gena was alone again with her thoughts. She curled up into a tight ball, hugging her knees and rocking back and forth. It was nice being able to see herself again, but tough not being able to see Twilight. Life was so full of give and take.

★ ★ ★

The week went by too quickly for Gena. She managed to avoid quips from Beth, who was spending all her snooty energy trying to get back at Nicole for deserting her. *Good,* Gena thought. I have other things to worry about. Like school and volleyball and tweezing my eyebrows for safe measure.

Once she considered riding her bike by Taylor's house to see if she could glimpse Twilight, then decided that it was a bad idea. She wondered why he didn't come back to the apartments. She really thought that first night he'd sneak back in like he had before, even though she never knew how he had managed to suddenly appear. But she knew it was final.

Waiting until the last minute, she slipped on the green dress, and for the first time, she saw herself wearing it. *Wow! Not bad, Richmond.* She resisted the urge to twirl the skirt back and forth in front of the mirror. She brushed her hair, and against all that she believed in, she applied some pale pink lipstick. *Almost clear,* she told herself. She stepped out of her bedroom to the sound of "Aww!" coming from Rachael and Dad.

Rachael wore a strapless, shell-colored gown, trimmed in pearls. Gena always thought of her as cute, but tonight she was beautiful. Even her pixie haircut was swooped in elegant waves.

And Dad! Gena had never seen him in a tux. He looked years younger. Then, just like in the fairy tales, the clock chimed. "Let's go," Dad said, jingling his car keys.

The ballroom was packed, mostly with white-haired couples in black tie and sequins. Gena glanced about. No boys her age. Good! Dressing up was one thing; dancing with a boy, forget it! She'd leave that little pleasure to Anne.

Rachael brought her some punch. "Enchanting, isn't it?"

"I guess," Gena said, not wanting to reveal how she really felt. "You look pretty tonight," she added. She knew her dad had told Rachael this a million times already, but she couldn't help noticing herself.

"Thanks," Rachael said, looking surprised. "And you're a vision yourself."

Gena shrugged. "I'd rather be wearing Dad's tee shirt."

Rachael winked. "Secretly, so would I!"

When Dad asked Rachael to dance, Gena found herself wandering in a sea of glittery people. She watched the orchestra for a minute, then stepped out onto the veranda to see the fountains. A girl dressed in pink chiffon shouted, "What are *you* doing here?"

Gena did a double-take. Beth! She resisted the urge to run. "What are *you* doing here?" she shot back.

"My father is the architect who designed this hospital. He's an important guest."

Gena shrugged. "My future stepmom works here. So get over it."

She turned quickly to get away, but that's when Mr. Wilson, Beth's father, emerged. "Beth, isn't this one of your little friends?"

Little? Before Gena could say, "Not on your life," he'd taken her by the arm and stood her next to Beth.

"You're both so breathtaking together." He lifted up an instant camera, and snapped a picture of the two of them. Gena blinked a few times, trying to remove the white spot from her eyes left by the flash. The film popped out with a whir, and he handed it to Beth. Someone caught his attention and led him off.

"Rip it up now and save yourself some time," Gena said.

But Beth fanned the film to help it develop faster. "No way! I have scissors at home. I'll just cut you out."

"Home?" Gena said. "Haven't you sold your house yet? Or are you planning to wheel it to Dallas too?"

Beth stuck up her nose. "Not going. Daddy said he couldn't leave. He has too much invested in Avery. This is our *home.*"

Wonderful, Gena thought, walking away. *A fairy tale? I'm in a bad soap opera!*

"Ahhhhhh!" Beth screamed. Gena whipped around in time to see her drop the photo on the ground and cover her mouth.

Finally got a good look at yourself? She went back without voicing the insult. Picking up the picture, she couldn't help but grin. Instead of her and Beth, standing side by side on a picturesque veranda, the photo showed Gena and Taylor, complete with plaid skirt and pigtails, peering through the mix-matched eyes of a cat.

"That's why I don't like you," Beth said. "You're so weird. All three of you!"

Gena couldn't help but grin. *Weird, huh?* She wouldn't have it any other way.

ABOUT DOTTI ENDERLE

Dotti Enderle is a Capricorn with E.S.P.—extra silly personality. She sleeps with the Three of Cups tarot card under her pillow to help her dream up new ideas for the Fortune Tellers Club. Dotti lives in Texas with her husband, two daughters, a cat, and a pesky ghost named Shakespeare. Learn more about Dotti and her books at:

www.fortunetellersclub.com

Here's a glimpse of what's ahead
in Fortune Tellers Club #7,
The Burning Pendulum

CHAPTER 2

Grave Dangers

"Aren't you going to say anything?" Anne asked.

Juniper leaned against the old magnolia tree in the school yard, wishing the bell would ring before Anne and Gena got into a tiff.

Gena still had a look of mild shock on her face. "Would you repeat that?" she asked. "I thought I heard you say that you like Kyle Morgan."

Anne slumped. "Come on, guys, you have to admit. He's gotten really cute."

"Kyle Morgan?" Gena asked, blinking and rattling her head. "As in a.k.a Booger Boy?"

Anne looked about ready to slug Gena with her backpack. "Oh, come on. That was in second grade!"

"And third, fourth, fifth . . . give me a break, Anne."

Juniper stepped in. "You really think he's cute, huh? I still can't get that booger-eating image out of my head."

"Have you seen him lately?" Anne asked.

"Yeah, he's let his hair grow out a little and combs it differently."

"I think he should comb it over his nose," Gena said. "That way we wouldn't have to see him pick his lunch."

"Fine," Anne said, turning her nose up slightly. "You won't have to see anyway. I'm sitting with him during lunch. You guys can sit across the room."

"Except that we have assigned tables," Gena smirked. "So you and Booger Boy sit at one end and we'll sit at another."

"I don't think we're being fair," Juniper said. She didn't want to sit away from Anne because of some boy. Especially Kyle Morgan who's reputation was built solely on immature snacking habits.

The bell rang before anything was solved. The girls headed toward the side doors of the school.

★ ★ ★

Juniper hated starting her day with mixed feelings. She woke up in a good mood, thinking about her dance solo for the school talent show next week, the extra bonus points she scored in science yesterday, and the missed classes tomorrow afternoon for the new library dedication ceremony. Things were great. Right? So why did she have a feeling they weren't?

There were only seven minutes left in first period when Juniper heard the beep of the intercom. She automatically knew the first storm clouds had rolled in.

"Would you send Juniper Lynch to the office, please?"

The class shuffled in their seats, watching her. She silently loaded her book and papers into her backpack and walked out. She didn't hurry, but she didn't slack either. How bad could it be? She'd never been in any real trouble in her life. Especially in school.

The principal's office smelled of lilac—or the dregs of an overpowering lilac perfume. Juniper preferred the stiff, leathery smell she had encountered the few times she'd been in here. Maybe the student who sat here before was called in from gym class, and did a fast stink-cover job with a bottle of cologne.

Mr. Chapman hurried in and sat down behind his desk. Juniper's heart jumped when she saw he was holding *Grave Dangers*.

"Juniper, I'm sorry to pull you out of class like this, but I just had a parent here who was quite upset."

Juniper sniffed the lilac air—definitely not a dad.

"She was upset about the book report you presented in English class yesterday."

"What did I do wrong?" Juniper asked, her voice cracking from nerves. She could see that Mr. Chapman was choosing his words carefully.

"It's not so much about right and wrong as it is about tastes . . . uh . . . and beliefs. This book you chose to do your report on, well, it contains some supernatural content."

Juniper relaxed. "So I'm not the only one in trouble." She thought about Jason Griggs doing his report on the third Harry Potter book. Who else reported on supernatural books yesterday? Her mind whirled to remember.

"You're not exactly in trouble, but your demonstration involved divination. Some people find that unsuitable, as does the school. Now I managed to calm this parent down with a simple agreement—that you'd pick a more appropriate book for the school library."

"But the teacher asked us to donate our favorite books," Juniper said, confused.

Mr. Chapman nodded. "I understand, but Juniper, let's not make a big deal over this, okay? I mean, it's just a flimsy paperback anyway." He bent back the spine and pages to demonstrate his point.

"I was going to donate more than one," Juniper offered, feeling strange about this whole thing.

Mr. Chapman rose and came around. Sitting down on the corner of his desk, he folded his hands and smiled. "You are one of our top students. Excellent grades, involved in school activities, and you show good citizenship."

She slumped. Nothing was worse than being talked down to by school authorities.

"So as a favor to me and yourself, choose another book."

Juniper nodded and rose. She forced a slight smile at Mr. Chapman and walked toward his office door. "Oh yeah—uh—sir? Can I have my book back?"

"It'll be here for you after school."

★ ★ ★

At lunch, Juniper didn't care that Kyle Morgan was sitting next to Anne at their usual lunch table. She scooted onto the bench across from them. Gena slid in next to her.

"I was called to the principal's office this morning," Juniper blurted.

Gena, Anne, and Kyle all stopped and stared. They looked at her like she'd sprouted horns and two extra eyes. She told the whole story while they unpacked their sandwiches, chips, and assorted sweets.

"That's stupid," Gena said, smooshing her peanut butter sandwich into a pancake-like treat. The imprint of her palm stayed on the bread.

"Yeah, it is," Juniper agreed, as she watched Gena roll the sandwich up and take a big bite. "But I don't want to make anyone mad."

"I think Psychic Circle is stupid," Kyle said, ripping the foil lid off his pudding.

Juniper sure didn't need his opinion. "It's not as stupid as eating your dessert first."

"At least it didn't come out of his schnozzle," Gena said.

Anne and Kyle both shot her a look with flame-thrower eyes.

"I just don't feel right about this," Juniper continued. "How come Jason can donate a Harry Potter book, but I can't donate mine?"

"Did you ask Mr. Chapman about that?" Anne asked.

"No, I was too chicken. Anyway, it's not fair."

Kyle dipped his finger in his pudding and brought out a big chocolate heap. "This is what I think of Psychic Circle." He smeared a giant brown streak across his tray."

"Have you ever read a Psychic Circle book?" Juniper asked.

"Heck, no! I'm not that dumb."

"Then how can you have an opinion about books you haven't read?"

Kyle licked the chocolate off his finger. "Get real. It's a group of teenagers who go around messing with astrology and feng shui and other fake junk. The whole idea is lame."

Juniper's blood grew warmer and she could feel her face grow flush. Anne squirmed a bit, not looking up. Before Juniper could speak, Gena jumped in.

"The whole idea of you being Anne's boyfriend is lame! It's obvious you don't have anything in common, other than she likes your new hair style. So just keep your opinions to yourself from now on, okay Booger Boy?"

Kyle aimed his juice box and squeezed, sending a stream of orange-pineapple liquid on Gena's face.

"Kyle!" Anne warned.

Gena snatched a stack of sour cream and onion potato chips and smashed them on top of Kyle's ketchup sandwich. "And here," she said, flinging a pickle chip that had fallen from Juniper's tuna. "Nice and juicy and green."

Juniper shut out their babyish behavior, feeling betrayed that Anne sat quietly, observing the fiasco, but not defending the Fortune Tellers Club. Kyle Morgan didn't have a right to smear her favorite series like he'd smeared the pudding. This day was getting worse by the minute—and it was only half over.

The Lost Girl
Fortune Tellers Club
Book 1
DOTTI ENDERLE

Twelve-year-old Juniper and her friends Anne and Gena call themselves the Fortune Tellers Club. For the past two years they've helped each other using Ouija boards, tarot cards, crystals, and other forms of divination.

When Gena misplaces her retainer, she turns to her friends for help. After several dead-end clues using the Ouija board, Juniper tries crystal gazing using a bowl of water. But instead of locating the retainer, she sees the gaunt face of a young girl.

The image is that of a missing child, nine-year-old Laurie Simmons. Now, the Fortune Tellers Club will stop at nothing, natural or supernatural, to find her.

0-7387-0253-6
144 pp., 5³⁄₁₆ x 7⁵⁄₈   **$4.99**

Playing with Fire
Fortune Tellers Club
Book 2
DOTTI ENDERLE

The second installment of the Fortune Tellers Club series crackles with suspense! Anne Donovan has a crush on Eric, the new boy at school. No one knows much about him except that he transferred schools after his house went up in flames.

Anne and her two friends, who call themselves The Fortune Tellers Club, spread the tarot cards to predict Anne's future as Eric's girlfriend. When a series of fires breaks out, including one that destroys the school library, their attention turns to a more burning question. Does Eric possesses a special power—pyrokinesis? They set to work searching for answers before everything around them turns to cinders.

0-7387-0340-0
5³⁄₁₆ x 7⁵⁄₈, 160 pp., 15 illus. $4.99

Magic Shades
Fortune Tellers Club
Book 3
DOTTI ENDERLE

Can Gena trust what she sees through those fifty-cent sunglasses? While rummaging through a resale shop, wisecracking tomboy Gena snatches up an enticing pair of mirrored cat-eye sunglasses.

Anne and Juniper, Gena's best friends and fellow members of the Fortune Tellers Club, don't exactly share Gena's enthusiasm for her new shades. They like them even less when they discover they are windows to the future, through which Gena can see things like the answers to her science test.

Are the glasses a blessing or a curse? When they show her dad's new girlfriend snooping in Gena's bedroom and her dad lying in a pool of blood in the kitchen, Gena's life takes an interesting turn.

0-7387-0341-9
144 pp., 5³⁄₁₆ x 7⁵⁄₈   **$4.99**

Secrets of Lost Arrow

Fortune Tellers Club
Book 4

DOTTI ENDERLE

It's Spring Break, and Juniper is boarding the bus with pals Gena and Anne to visit her grandmother, Nana, in the town of Lost Arrow. On the first day, the girls explore the graveyard next to Lightfoot Creek. There they meet Cody, a local boy, who knows all the secret hideaways and local legends. He tells them things about Nana—things that Juniper doesn't want to believe.

Nana is behaving strangely. Come evening, a mysterious fog creeps up to the house, and Nana's mood changes. When Juniper wakes in the middle of the night to find Nana missing, her curiosity gets the best of her. She follows a glowing light to the cemetery, and there the startling truth about Nana is revealed.

0-7387-0389-3
160 pp., 5³⁄₁₆ x 7⅝, illus. $4.99

Hand of Fate
Fortune Tellers Club
Book 5
DOTTI ENDERLE

Are the fates conspiring against Anne?

A car accident prevents Anne from going to cheer-leader camp and possibly winning the Cheerleader of the Year Award. This odd twist of events provokes the Fortune Tellers Club to explore the cause of the accident.

Using astrology and other fortune telling techniques, the girls discover a strange connection between Anne and a woman she's never met. As the club gradually unravels the tangled web of fate, Anne learns shocking news about herself. Anne can't help asking if fate forced her to miss cheerleading camp. And, if so, why?

0-7387-0390-7
144 pp., 5³⁄₁₆ x 7⁵⁄₈   **$4.99**